Yuzi's False Alarm

Secret Keeper
GIRL

*Other books in the
Secret Keeper Girl Series*

Yuzi's False Alarm

Dannah Gresh
author of Secret Keeper Girl

and Chizuruoke Anderson

Moody Publishers

CHICAGO

Interior design: JuliaRyan | www.DesignByJulia.com
Cover and illustrations: Andy Mylin
Some images: © 2008 JupiterImages Corporation

Library of Congress Cataloging-in-Publication Data

Gresh, Dannah.
 Yuzi's false alarm / by Dannah Gresh and Chizuruoke Anders ;
[illustrations by Andy Mylin].
   p. cm. -- (Secret Keeper Girl series)
 Summary: Sixth-grader Yuzi, trying hard to fit in at a new school, is traumatized by being asked to dress as a stalk of corn in the town's annual Popcorn Festival and soon finds herself in after-school detention, where she meets three other girls who join her in forming the "Secret Keeper Girl Club." Includes a mother/daughter Girl Gab assignment.
 ISBN 978-0-8024-8704-9
[1. Clubs--Fiction. 2. Middle schools--Fiction. 3. Schools--Fiction. 4. Moving, Household--Fiction. 5. Christian life--Fiction. 6. Friendship--Fiction.] I. Anderson, Chizuruoke. II. Mylin, Andy, ill. III. Title.
 PZ7.G8633Yuz 2008
 [Fic]--dc22

                            2008026488

We hope you like this book from Moody Publishers. We want to give you books that help you think and figure out what truth really looks like. If you liked this and want more information, you and/or your mom can go to www.moodypublishers.com or write to . . .

Moody Publishers
820 N. LaSalle Boulevard
Chicago, IL 60610

1 3 5 7 9 10 8 6 4 2

Printed in the United States of America

To D.A., my love, and S.A., my smile.

C.A.

CHAPTER 1

Under Corn-struction

This is not happening! This is NOT happening! I feel all prickly from head to toe—and not because it's a hot day, either. Here I am totally sprawled on the ground with no hope of saving a scrap of dignity or I-meant-to-do-that-ness. Why can't the warm ground split open and swallow me whole?

Maybe if I lie here perfectly still, no one will notice me. No one will notice the girl lying facedown dressed in a tight, itchy, horrible corncob costume!

Yes. I am dressed as a **cob of corn**.

This was not my idea. It's all part of my mom's twisted plan to help me feel welcome here in Marion, Ohio, which happens to be "The Popcorn Capital of the World." My family just moved here one week, six days, and thirteen hours ago because of Dad's job. Mom figured it would be a good idea for me to be a greeter at the town's annual Popcorn Festival. No big deal, *except* I had to dress from head to toe in bright green and yellow spandex! This is definitely not the best way to make a good impression in a new town. I know I'm feeling sorry for myself. But I should! Nobody else seems to be too bothered by the fact that I was volunteered, without being asked, to be a corny greeter.

When I came home from school earlier today to find the corncob costume lying on the couch, I asked my mom the obvious question, "What is *that*?"

"It's for you to wear when we go to the Popcorn Festival this afternoon," she told me. "I met a new friend today. Her name is Sue Kenworth and she is in charge of the greeters for the festival. One got sick, so she needs someone to fill in for her at one of the entrances. I told her you'd be glad to do it."

It all started to make horrible sense.

"Me?? *I'm* supposed to *wear* it?" My voice had gone so high, I was squealing. But I didn't care. "How am I supposed to get my hair in there?!"

Well, my hair *is* in there. And now, me and my hair can't wait to get out of this suit. I'm **never** gonna forgive Mom for this!

The stiff corn husks made it really difficult to get vertical again. When I finally got up, I ignored all the concerned faces looking at me. My nose is doing that tickly thing it does when I'm about to cry.

Don't you dare cry, I tell myself.

The only thing worse than being stuck in a corncob costume at a festival in a new town is bawling your eyes out in a corncob costume at a festival in a new town. I clenched my jaw, but one stubborn tear slipped out anyway.

"Well, hello. You must be the new girl in town!" The voice came from a super-smiley lady with lime-green glasses. Her short red hair was sticking out in every direction. On purpose, I think. I pretended to scratch the corner of my eye as I quickly wiped away the tear.

"Thanks for helping out today," she said, squinting in the sun. I assumed she was the woman who got me into this unfortunate comedy. "What's your name again, hon?"

"Yuzi," I answered.

"What?"

"Yuzi," I repeated.

"You're woozy? No wonder, in that getup!" She laughed.

"No. Yuzi," I said, slowly. "*Y-u-z-i.*"

"Ohhh, Yooozy! Where*ever* did you get a name like that?" Spiky Red asked, grinning.

I took a deep breath and started to explain. "My full name is Uzoma Ukachi. It's Nigerian. Most people can't pronounce it, so my nickname is just the first two letters of my first name: *u-z*. And I spell it *Y-u-z-i*. Yuzi."

"Woo! That was a mouthful! I have never been sooo happy to hear someone has a nickname. I'm Sue. No story. Just Sue Kenworth." She stuck out her hand to shake mine, and then laughed like someone had told a funny joke. "It is hot to-*day*. But that probably doesn't bother you since you're from Africa. I, on the other hand, feel like I'm melting," Sue said, fanning herself with her hand.

People usually assume I can handle any kind of heat because I'm Nigerian. But hot is hot. Besides, I'm wearing a spandex corncob.

"My son's around here someplace," Sue said, looking around. "I'd love for him to meet you."

I tried to stop her. "Oh, no . . . that's okay . . . I don't really . . ."

"I don't see Trevor anywhere. He'll be so sad he missed you," she said with a sigh.

I smiled sympathetically, but inside I was relieved.

"Where are you going to school, Yuzi?" Sue asked.

"Rutherford B. Hayes Middle School."

"Oh, that's perfect! You'll probably run into Trevor there. Maybe you'll be in some of the same classes," Sue said excitedly. She looked at her watch. "I've got to run. But it was so nice talking to you. See you around, all right?"

I nodded and smiled.

"By the way," she said, winking like we shared a special secret, "you speak very good English." She waved, and then disappeared into the crowd.

I waved back limply. I'm getting used to that weird compliment. So many people I've met think that if I'm African, and my name is African, then English must be difficult for me. But it's not. In my family, we speak to each other a lot in Ibo, a Nigerian language. But of course, when we speak to anyone else, we use English.

I looked around, wondering where my family was. They were probably walking around, visiting different booths, and having a grand time dressed as *people*. I sighed. I hadn't even asked Mrs. Kenworth when my torture would be over. A person can only handle so many hugs from cranky, sticky toddlers.

I heard familiar voices behind me and turned to see my dad, mom, two sisters, and little brother standing there with their hands full of hot, roasted corn on the cob,

GO TO
secretkeepergirl.com
and type in the secret
word "Ibo" to learn
some Ibo!

towering ice cream cones, glistening hot dogs on soft buns, clouds of cotton candy in rainbows of color, and, of course, buckets of buttery popcorn. I grabbed a handful of Dad's popcorn and shoved it into my mouth.

My mom said, "Hello, dear! We just saw Sue and she said you'll be done in about fifteen minutes."

"Good," I said. "I feel like I've been wearing this forever." I still wasn't sure if I planned to forgive my mom and dad for ruining my life by moving me to this literally corny town. I did know the chances were slim that I'd recover from this traumatic start.

"But you look great—and leafy," my six-year-old brother, Ike, said, grinning mischievously. His real name is Ikechukwu, but most people call him Ike so they don't choke on his full name. His tongue was blue from his giant puff of cotton candy.

I rolled my eyes.

"Bye," I said pitifully as they walked away.

There's got to be a way for me to make friends in this new place, but I'm pretty sure it won't happen while I'm wearing *this* outfit.

I tried to make an effort for the last ten minutes. I smiled widely and put up with more hugs. Then, just as

I saw Mrs. Kenworth coming toward me again, my left foot somehow caught my right foot, and—yeah—I was on the ground again.

Lately, it's like my body's not mine. It's as if someone gave me a new collection of muscles and forgot to leave a manual. Mom says I'm going through a major growth spurt, as if moving to a new town isn't enough for me to deal with.

Sue hurriedly helped me up, concerned. "Are you all right, Yuzi?"

"Growth spurt," I mumbled, humiliated yet again.

She looked at me with a puzzled expression.

Not wanting to be rude but dying to get out of there, I asked quietly, "Am I done?"

"Absolutely yes. You were a lifesaver. Fantastic job. Thank you so much!" she said. "I'll be by next week to pick up the costume. Are you sure you're all right?"

"Yes, I'm fine. Thanks. See ya." And I stalked off toward our van. Yes, *stalked*. And it's **not** funny.

I think I'm going to hate this town.

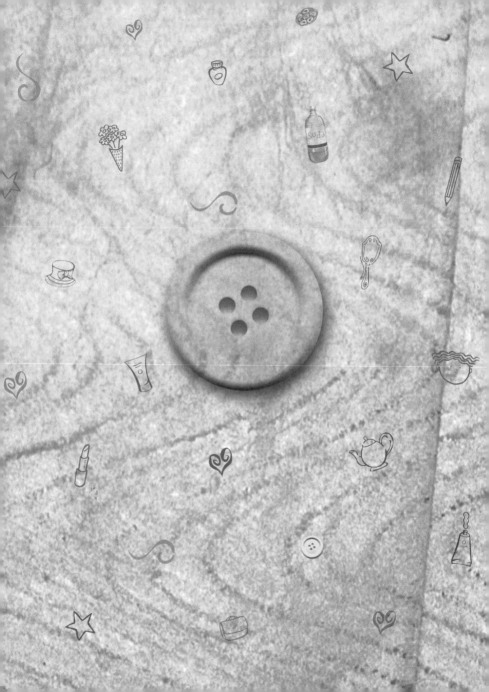

Yuzi's False Alarm

CHAPTER 2

An Angry Ostrich

"Two thousand forty-two ostriches. Two thousand forty-three ostriches. Two thousand forty-four ostriches . . ."

This is how I stayed awake Sunday night. I figured that if counting sheep helps a person fall asleep, then maybe counting something else might help me stay awake. I chose ostriches.

If you stay awake for most of the night, it seems to slow down the coming of the next day—which was good for me. But it also gives you a lot of time to think—which was bad for me. By the time my mom came in to wake me up this miserable Monday morning, my head felt like it would explode and my eyeballs were on fire. I lay there, slowly rolling my eyes around. *Ow. Burny.*

Mom came into my room to see if I was awake, and could immediately tell I had not slept well.

"Uzoma, you look so tired. Are you still worried about school today?" Mom asked.

I squinted back at her like the room was smoky.

"I'm worried because of how Thursday and Friday went. What if the school *still* has my classes all mixed up? I hate having to constantly switch classes and teachers!" I said, hoping she'd feel sorry for me and let me stay home for the rest of my life.

"Everything about your classes will be worked out. You'll see. It'll be fine." She hugged me. "Now, go get ready."

She was speaking to me in Ibo, which totally calms me down—normally. But nothing seemed to be breaking through the fuzz around my brain this morning.

As I was brushing my teeth, the knot in my stomach tightened. I tried to ignore it, but my thoughts were in a knot, too.

My mom wasn't right about me liking this town. What if she's not right about making friends? What if I don't ever make any friends?

What if they think I dress funny? Of course, according to the corncob costume I wore on Friday, I *do* dress funny.

I spit into the sink.

Maybe I don't feel well, I thought, staring into the mirror. In old cartoons, people always check their tongues for spots when they're sick. I stuck my tongue out really far. No spots. Not a one.

As I stepped into the shower, my six-year-old sister, Peace, opened the bathroom door and came in. She's Ike's twin, older by ninety seconds. And she doesn't let him forget it.

"Peace! I've told you like a zillion times . . . you need to knock!" I said, really annoyed.

"Sorry," she chirped.

Peace looked like a blurry blob through the shower curtain, but I could totally tell *she* was excited about school. Oh, to be six again . . .

"Striped one or the purple one?" she asked.

"What?" I asked. I hadn't been listening. Besides, with the shower running and her mouth full of toothpaste foam, it was hard to understand what she was saying. Peace started to repeat herself.

"Spit out first. I can't understand you," I said.

She spit. "My skirt. Should I wear the striped one or the purple?"

"What top?" I asked.

"My orange shirt with the sparkly fish on the front," she said.

"Striped," I answered.

"What are *you* going to wear?" she asked.

"No idea," I muttered.

"That's okay," she said matter-of-factly. "You look

great in anything." And she bounced out of the bathroom.

I really do have a sweet little sis. Too bad I can't just hang out with her all day instead of going to school.

At school, the faded smell of textbooks and floor cleaner greeted me. I could hear my heartbeat louder than my footsteps as the shiny hallway floor stretched out in front of me. I was being led to my new class by Principal Butter. No joke. His name really is Principal *Butter*.

I followed him to Language Arts. Hopefully this was the last switch.

"So, how long did you live in Nigeria?" Principal Butter asked.

"Well, actually," I explained, "I've never lived in Nigeria, but my parents are Nigerian. I was born in Texas, then we moved around a lot. But before we moved here, we lived in London, England."

"Very interesting . . . well, I'm sure you're going to really enjoy your new LA teacher. Her name's Mrs. Chickory," he said.

Mrs. Chickory is tall, but with really small feet. Her head is small, but she has the hugest black eyes with dark, bushy eyebrows and a super-weird, almost beaklike nose. She reminds me . . . of something . . .

Oh, yeah! The ostriches I was counting last night, I thought as she walked toward me. I could picture her strutting around in my ostrich-counting mind. She put one feathery wing, er, arm around my shoulders.

"Welcome to our class," Mrs. Chickory said loudly.

She smelled a little like cream of broccoli soup. I could imagine her bending down to slurp it, ignoring the spoon.

"Class, this is Yuzi," she said as if she had rescued me from some other LA class.

I heard the whole class repeat my name in giggly whispers. How embarrassing.

"She is new to our school and is all the way from Nigeria," she said. "Please make her feel welcome."

Great. Whenever I'm introduced that way, people think I flew in from Nigeria just this morning and can't speak a word of English.

Mrs. Chickory pointed the way to my desk. "Larissa, Yuzi is going to sit next to you so you can help her out. Okay?"

Larissa smiled at me, and I was relieved to finally sit down. I was pulling a notebook out of my bag when Larissa leaned over to me. She has big brown eyes and she opened them even wider as she said, "Will you be my African friend? I've never had an African friend before."

What am I? Some sort of a *collectible doll*? I pictured myself packaged in a box for sale in the Barbie aisle.

Before I had a chance to respond, Mrs. Chickory's sharp voice said, "Yuzi, although you're new here, I want you to know that the one thing I do not tolerate in class is talking without permission."

"I wasn't," I said in a totally defensive voice. I felt hot all over.

"I also expect my students to apologize when they've made a mistake, not deny it," Mrs. Chickory continued.

"But I **wasn't** talking!" It came out louder than I meant it to, but I couldn't help it. I was being accused of something I didn't do! "All I did was sit down and start getting my stuff out. Larissa asked me a quick question and I hadn't even answered her yet."

"Young lady," Mrs. Chickory interrupted me. She pressed her lips into a straight line, which made her look like an *angry* ostrich.

"I don't know what they do in Nigeria, but here in America we respect our authorities! I'm going to ask you to step out into the hall for a few minutes and calm yourself. Wait out there until I say you can join the class again," she said, obviously really mad.

I stood up slowly. My heart was pounding and my throat

was tight. All the students were looking at me as I made my way to the door.

I was only in the class for like five minutes. I didn't do anything wrong! If all these terrible things keep happening to me, no one's *ever* going to know the real me.

I squeezed my eyes shut, holding back tears. With my back against a locker in the empty hall, I slowly slid to the floor, pulled my knees up to my chest, and wrapped my arms around them. As I dropped my head down, the shrill, brain-jangling sound of the fire alarm ripped through the silence. I jumped up, eyes wide, and slammed my hands over my ears. Out of the corner of my eye, I saw someone round the corner out of the hallway.

The horrible alarm continued as Mrs. Chickory dashed into the hall. She looked at me, then at the pulled fire alarm on the wall only a few lockers away. Her eyes returned to me and narrowed into slits. Then it hit me. She thought I pulled the alarm!

Students were flooding into the halls on their way to the exits. As Mrs. Chickory's class passed by, she frowned hard at me and said tightly, "You're coming with me."

She started to strut down the hall, assuming I would follow her.

I'm gonna hate this school.

Yuri's False Alarm

CHAPTER 3

Chickory, Buttery, Flop

"You *need* to understand me. Please! I didn't pull that alarm!" I said for the hundredth time. I was flipping out.

"We understand what you're saying, Yuzi, but you were the only one in the hallway," Principal Butter said.

I was sitting on the edge of a chair across from his desk. It felt really hot in there, but I was shivering. My mouth was so dry that I could hardly swallow. Mom was sitting next to me, hands together against her lips. Mrs. Chickory towered behind us, balanced on her tiny ostrich feet.

Principal Butter grabbed a bunch of tissues and wiped the sweat from his shiny head. Tiny shreds of tissue clung to his scalp. Through tear-blurred eyes, he looked like he had dots of toothpaste all over his head. For one weird moment, I felt a giggle coming up in my throat. If I weren't in the middle of the worst situation of my life, I might have busted up laughing. But I was in the principal's office. And this was no laughing matter.

"I wasn't the only one in the hallway!" I said. "There was someone else."

"Who? Would you be able to identify them?" Principal Butter asked.

"I didn't get a good look," I said.

"Boy or girl?" he asked.

"I'm not sure. I saw they were wearing jeans, and I think it looked like a boy's shoe," I said, knowing it sounded dumb because it seems like practically the entire school is in jeans. "And there was a whitish mark on the bottom of one shoe," I added.

Mrs. Chickory made a funny snorting sound behind me. I looked back. Her chin was tipped up a little, and one raised eyebrow seemed to say, "I told you so" to the principal.

"When I stepped out into the hallway, Principal Butter, there was no one there except Yuzi," said Mrs. Chickory impatiently. "And as I've already told you, she was sporting quite an attitude when she left the classroom."

"But you didn't actually *see* her pull the alarm," said Principal Butter.

"Well, no. But she was standing right there!" Mrs. Chickory kind of sounded like Ike when he's whining for more dessert.

"Thank you, Mrs. Chickory. I apologize for keeping you so long. You can return to your class," Principal Butter said.

I could feel Mrs. Chickory staring at the back of my head, like sunlight through a magnifying glass. I could almost hear the sizzling sound. Then she left the office.

Principal Butter breathed in deeply. "This is most unfortunate, Mrs. Ukachi," he said to my mom. "Pulling a fire alarm is an extremely disruptive and expensive prank."

"I don't believe that my daughter would do such a thing. It's just not like her," Mom said. "She's also not prone to lying. If she says there was someone else in that hallway, I believe there was."

"I understand, Mrs. Ukachi, but no one else saw this supposed 'other person.'" Principal Butter made quote signs in the air with his fingers, then took another deep breath. "This is what I'll do. I'm sure this move has been difficult enough as it is, so, because Yuzi is so new here, I won't suspend her." He laced his fingers together and looked at me. "But it *does* look as if she pulled that alarm. And unless this other person confesses, or Yuzi can

27

identify him or her, I'm afraid I have no choice but to put her in after-school detention for three days beginning this Wednesday."

The office was completely silent, except for the scratch of a pen scribbling and then a little sliding sound as Principal Butter pushed the pink slip across his desk toward me.

I picked it up by the tippiest tip of a corner, like someone had used it to blow their nose.

Once I was in the hall alone with Mom, I let out all the things that were yelling inside my head.

"Detention for three days?" I said. "I'm getting detention for something I didn't do! This is **so** unfair! Mom, I hate this town. I hate this school. I hate my life! I can never forgive you for moving me here!"

Mom just listened and rubbed my back.

"This is not going to help my 'new girl' problem one tiny bit. I had no friends to begin with, and now my reputation is crumbling like a sad sandcastle!" I paused. "Oh, that's right!" I said. "I don't even *have* a reputation yet. Unless you can count 'spandex-corncob-wearing-fire-alarm-psycho-freak!'"

My mom looked at me softly. "I know it's not right, but sometimes we have to endure things that aren't fair. And even though it hurts, it can make us stronger."

So I'll be lonely, but at least I'll be *strong*?

Oh, yay.

After dinner, Dad said he and Mom wanted to talk to me.

"So," Dad began. He and Mom and I were in their room with the door closed. In my house a closed door equals serious conversation.

Dad was sitting on the edge of the bed, resting against the headboard. He looked at me and continued, "So, I hear you're spending some time in detention for something you didn't do and it's your mom's and my fault for moving you to this horrible place."

When he put it that way, I sounded pretty terrible. He took the wind right out of my angry sails.

I shrugged. "It's so unfair," I mumbled softly. Then louder, "I can't believe I'm going to be punished for something I didn't do! Can't you think of some brilliant plan to get me out of this, Dad? You're a super-brainy geophysicist!"

Dad just smiled and shook his head.

I continued, "Ever since we moved to Marion, my life's been like some kind of whirling merry-go-round of craziness! Somebody needs to stop the ride or I'm gonna **puke!**"

"Uzoma, *wodata obi u ala,*" Mom said gently. She says that whenever I start freaking out over something. It means "settle your heart down," which really means that I need to get a grip. She'd been pretty patient with my angry accusations. Now, I could feel her reeling me in.

"Seriously, Mom! Things just keep getting worse and worse! Some psycho kid at that crazy school pulled that fire alarm and knows that I got in trouble for it and doesn't even care! Grrrrr!" I crossed my arms across my chest. "I have *got* to find that kid and when I do . . . !"

"I'm sure whoever did it knows they did the wrong thing," Mom said. "It's quite possible that they feel bad, but are too frightened to confess."

"Mom! I can't believe you're defending someone who did this to me," I said. "You should be helping me blow their cover and send their sorry popcorn-popping self to the Butter Principal!"

"Okay," Dad said, getting up from the bed. "We'll just take everything one day at a time." He hugged me. "Go take care of your homework."

Mom came over and gave me a hug, too. I knew I didn't deserve it.

"And don't worry," Mom said. "These awful events won't last forever. You'll make friends, and have fun. Who knows? You might even start to like it here." She winked and smiled.

"U-girl, you might stop looking at what everyone else is doing wrong and start trying to see what lesson you're supposed to learn in all of this," my dad challenged tenderly.

I got off the bed and left their bedroom.

They just don't understand, I thought.

What *I* didn't understand is that I actually did have a reputation already. I just didn't know it.

Yuzi's False Alarm

CHAPTER 4

Detention Convention

On Wednesday, the day of my first-ever detention, Rutherford B. Hayes Middle School rang with a unique sound. And it wasn't a fire alarm. It was the chorus of names being woven into the song of my new reputation at my new school in my new town.

Everywhere I went, kids made comments about me and the fire alarm. One boy named Brock actually tried to *congratulate* me at lunch.

"Hey!" he said with his mouth full. "You're *that* girl!"

I could see chewed-up chips and hot dog mingling together in his mouth. **Gross**.

Brock is shaped like an eggplant—round, but not flabby. And not purple. His hair looked like he'd just gotten out of bed . . . and not in that cool, skater-boy kind of way.

"Sweet job on that fire alarm!" he continued. And he raised one hand for a high five.

As he said the word "fire," a soggy chunk of chewed chip hit me right near my mouth. *Eew, eew, eew, eew!* I silently panicked.

Instead of high-fiving him back, I quickly grabbed my napkin and wiped my cheek. I wiped so hard, it felt like skin was going to come off. He didn't even notice.

"I didn't pull the fire alarm," I said, annoyed.

"Whatever you say, Ding-Dong!" Brock said, mimicking the sound of the fire alarm. He popped his eyebrows up and down while grinning, and elbowed me in the arm a couple times. Of course he didn't believe me. Nobody believes me.

"Don't call me that!" I said.

"No problem, Ding-Dong!" he said, smiling. "See ya around!"

Why do boys talk so loudly? There is no way I'm going to live with a nickname like that or the other ones being pinned on me. I have to find the real culprit and stick a few names on him.

But first I have to survive detention.

As the school emptied at the end of the day, I made my way to Mrs. Velasquez's art room. The art room isn't the usual place for detention, and Mrs. Velasquez isn't the usual detention teacher. The rumor is that some girl threw her lunch at the regular detention teacher, Mrs. Hefty, a couple days ago. Everyone is saying that Mrs. Hefty's face turned blue from the impact and that's why she's out for the week.

As I walked in, I got a whiff of something wonderful. The crayon-glue-paint-clay smell of the art room is one of my very favorite smells in the whole world. Almost better than my mom making fried plantains. It made me feel a little better. A *little*.

Mrs. Velasquez was sitting at a desk near the front of the room. She's really pretty. She smiled at me. A real smile, like we knew each other. I handed her my pink slip. She signed it and handed it back. "I'm Mrs. V," she said.

"I didn't pull it," I said suddenly. "The fire alarm. It wasn't me." I felt it was important that she know that.

"Well, who did it?" Mrs. V asked pleasantly.

"I'm not sure. But I'm sure going to find out," I said.

"I hope you find the culprit." Then she made a sweeping motion with her arm and said, "Feel free to use anything in the room."

I looked at her, surprised. I hadn't been in detention

35

before, but I was pretty sure you weren't supposed to walk around, using what you liked.

Mrs. V, seeing my hesitation, said, "I know that's not how detention normally is, but this week is a little different, and you're in my art room. So go ahead. Use what you want."

Maybe this won't be so bad after all.

I got a large piece of cream-colored paper, some wide-tip markers, and some colored pencils. Then I sat down at a table in the back of the room.

There were three other girls in detention besides me—a reddish-blonde-haired girl, an Asian girl, and a really tall brown-haired girl who looked a little like Mrs. V. Of course, I had no idea who they were or why they were here.

I decided I was going to make a list of all the terrible things that had happened to me in the last week. I used different shades of blue for all the rotten things:

1. MOVED!!!
I wrote that in really angry letters!

2. WIPED OUT . . . IN GREEN SPANDEX!
I used a greenish-blue for that one.

3. Not sure when to forgive Mom and Dad. Maybe never.

4. The Ostrich

I figured that pretty much said it all for my LA teacher. I selected a crazy-bright color for the really, really rottenest thing ever. Maybe it would seem less horrible written in Sunburst Orange.

5. Fire Alarm!

The clock was ticking slowly. So I decided to use the colored pencils to draw little pictures next to my new list. It made me laugh to draw a picture of Mrs. Chickory next to "The Ostrich!"

When I got down to the fire alarm problem, I had an idea. Maybe if I could just concentrate on what I saw in the hall, I'd be able to remember more details. I sketched as much as I could possibly remember about the jeans and the shoe and the mark on the sole.

I squeezed my eyes shut, searching for more details. Then I felt a hand on my arm. I jumped and my eyes flew open.

"Whoa. Didn't mean to scare you," said the tall girl. She must have walked over while I was concentrating on my list.

"I didn't know if you were okay," she said.

"Oh! Yeah, I'm okay. I was just thinking . . . really hard," I said.

"No kidding. You didn't even hear me walk up," the girl said. Then she smiled. Standing beside me, she was even taller than I thought. Her dark, curly hair was pulled back in a slick ponytail.

"I'm Toni," she said, smiling.

"I'm Yuzi," I said, smiling back.

"Fire alarm chick?" Toni said, laughing.

"I didn't do it." I've been saying that a lot lately. "There was someone else in the hall with me, but I didn't get a good look."

"What?!" Toni said, shocked. "Then what're you in here for?"

"Well, I can't identify who it was, and nobody seems to believe I saw anyone at all," I said.

"That is **so** totally unfair!" Toni said. She plopped down onto a seat next to me. "You have to figure out who you saw. Is that what you were concentrating on a couple minutes ago?" She tilted her head to look at my paper. "Wow. You can really draw."

"Thanks," I said, slowly folding up the brightly colored

sheet on my desk. I didn't feel like having someone else read my "List of Terribles" just yet.

"The thing is, I saw the person who did it . . . or at least part of him. I saw his shoe as he was running around the corner. I know it was a boy's sneaker, and it had some kind of a mark on the bottom of it," I explained.

"What kind of mark?" Toni asked.

39

"Well, that's my other problem. I hardly saw it. It was a light-colored symbol, or something, on a black sole. But it wasn't very clear." I thought hard. "It was kind of like a . . . circle, maybe, but not colored in. A sort of wavy circle."

"Did it look like the guy drew it on there, or was it part of the shoe?" Toni asked.

"I think it might have been drawn," I said slowly. "Maybe."

Toni chewed the inside of her left cheek, thinking. "I still can't believe you're in here," she said, shaking her head. "That's just not right."

Just then, the girl at Mrs. V's desk (I think I heard Mrs. V call her Kate) called out to the other girl.

"Danika, tell Mrs. V your idea about the *Secret Keeper Girl Club!*" And she waved her hand to have Danika join her at Mrs. V's desk. Kate seems uber-perky.

Danika is the "Lunch-Thrower." I figured that out while I was writing my list. She has glossy, stick-straight black hair, and there wasn't a thing out of place from the top of her pink headband to her sparkly pink toenails. She really doesn't look like someone who would toss her lunch at a teacher.

Come to think of it, none of the girls in the room seemed like they should be there.

Toni and I kind of listened in as Danika told Mrs. V about her idea for a girls' club. The club would be a place where girlfriends could talk about what they're going through and know their problems wouldn't be blabbed about. A club of true friends that you trust and who look out for you.

I most definitely could use a club like that right about . . . let me see . . . now! I thought. This whole friendless thing was getting really old really fast.

Kate and Danika talked to Mrs. V quietly for a few more minutes. I felt pretty left out. It was obvious that they didn't want Toni and me to hear them.

What happened next seemed way too perfect. All three of them came over to Toni and me and just outright asked if we wanted to be part of the *Secret Keeper Girl Club*.

"Yes!" I blurted out, surprising myself. Then I added slowly, "Yes, I'll do it!"

Toni agreed to be part of the club, too. I introduced myself for real to Kate and Danika. They said we would meet once a week, on Wednesdays after school, here in Mrs. V's art room.

Was it possible that I'd just moved from friendless, spandex-wearing, fire-alarm-chick to an actual member of the social network of sixth grade at Rutherford B. Hayes Middle School? Of course, it was a little strange that I found the *Secret Keeper Girl Club* and three new friends in detention. Strange, but *totally* cool.

Now, I just needed to find the guy who actually pulled that fire alarm. I can't wait to wrap my fingers around his creepy little neck.

If only I could remember that crazy shape drawn on his black-soled shoe . . .

Yuzi's False Alarm

CHAPTER 5

Hiccups and Minivans

I never knew you could get hiccups that could actually lift you off your seat.

A boy sitting next to me in science class had the hiccups of all hiccups. It sounded like an enormous toad had been set loose in the classroom. Of course, the class completely cracked up laughing.

"Trevor, is there a problem?" asked Mr. Picadilly.

"I have (CROAK!) the hiccups, Mr. Pic—(CROAK!)," Trevor tried to answer.

"Good gracious, Trevor! Those aren't hiccups; they sound more like a cry of alarm from an alien life form!" Mr. Picadilly exclaimed.

Then the class really fell apart. Mr. Picadilly is a funny teacher. He makes the craziest faces when he's explaining the food chain of the rain forest.

"Go get some water!" Mr. Picadilly said to Trevor.

Trevor's face was as red as his hair, but he was grinning as he left the room.

There were only a few minutes left in class, and Mr. Picadilly said we could talk quietly. So when Trevor came back to his seat, I turned to him and said, "Those were insane! Have you always hiccupped like that?"

"Yeah," Trevor said. "Forever and ever. It rocks!"

"You *do* know who that is, don't you?" A familiar voice from behind cut into our conversation. We both turned. It was Brock—without food in his mouth, thank goodness.

"That's Ding-Dong!" Brock continued excitedly.

Trevor didn't even look confused. He knew what Brock was referring to, I guessed.

"Back off, Brock," Trevor said, surprising me.

"I'm just sayin'!" Brock said, and scooched back in his seat.

I rolled my eyes.

"I don't get why so many kids think I'm cool because of the whole fire alarm thing," I said. "It drives me crazy because I didn't do it! And nobody believes me!"

"Yeah," he mumbled and then changed the subject. "So . . . um . . . you're from Africa, huh? Jambo! That's all I know."

"'Hello' is just fine, especially since 'jambo' is Swahili, and I am a Nigerian who was born in Texas," I said.

"Oh," Trevor said. "So what's with your name, anyway?"

I explained—again. I am *always* explaining my name. I should totally come up with a card or something that I can hand to people when they ask. It could seriously save time.

"Whoa," he said when I finished. "And I'm just Trevor. No story."

Where have I heard that before? I thought. Then I remembered. *Red hair! That lady from the Popcorn Festival!*

"What's your last name?" I asked.

"Kenworth," he said.

"No way!" I said. "You're Sue Kenworth's son! I should have known by your hair."

"How do you know my mom?" he asked.

"Ummmm . . . I met her at the Popcorn Festival," I said truthfully, but avoiding any exposure of my day in the corncob suit.

"Oh yeah," Trevor said as he thought about it. "I kind of remember her saying something about some girl. Weren't you dressed up, or something?"

"Never mind," I said quickly.

The bell rang, and the whole class moved toward the door like a herd of cows.

45

"See you later," I said to Trevor.

"Yeah," he answered, and popped his chin in my general direction.

He seemed nice enough.

After detention that afternoon, Toni and I were waiting outside for my mom to pick me up. Toni was going to come home with me so we could figure out how to find the shoe guy.

"Hey, Trevor," I said, as my new boy-bud walked by in a football uniform.

"Hey," he said back. Then he locked eyes with Toni, who had frozen beside me.

They glared at each other silently for about two seconds. Then Trevor pushed past us.

"Whoa! What was *that*?" I asked. "I think I saw smoke coming out of your ears."

"Long story," Toni said. "The short version is that Trevor is a slimeball that's too thick-headed to know when he's been beat."

One thing I'd learned really quickly is that Toni is crazy into sports and super competitive. She actually landed in detention for trying out for the boys' football

46

team, which is totally against school rules! Now, I was learning that she sure didn't like Trevor.

"Wow," I said. "I met him today in Social Studies. He's just about the only person who didn't ask me about the fire alarm." I shrugged. "He seems nice."

"You can't be serious," Toni said, making a face like she had smelled roadkill. "I can think of a whole bunch of words to describe Trevor Kenworth, and 'nice' isn't one of them!"

"Whoa! Chill out, *chica!*" I said, kind of joking.

Mom pulled her tan minivan up to the curb beside us and I jumped in first, making room for Toni.

I gave a quick introduction to my sisters and brother. An Alayna Rayne song blared from the radio. She's amazing and my brother and sisters like her, too. Peace and Ike started yelling and Patience was doing a crazy little wiggle dance in her car seat. Toni and I sang along, using the pencils in our hands as microphones.

When the song ended, we laughed and caught our breath in a moment of silence.

Peace suddenly asked, "Have you come up with a way to find the shoe guy?"

"What shoe guy?" Ike asked.

"The fire alarm person. The one who really pulled it," Peace said to Ike.

"We haven't come up with any good ideas yet," I said, looking at Toni and shrugging.

"I've been thinking," Peace continued. "How about making everyone crawl around on their hands and knees so you can see the bottoms of their shoes?"

"How would I get them to do that?" I asked.

"Tell them it's Somersault Day!" Ike said.

"Pretend you're all in caves!" Peace said.

"Stop, drop, and roll!" Ike shouted. "Like in a fire!"

"That doesn't make any sense," Peace said, crossing her arms.

"Your little sibs are creative creatures," Toni said.

"Throw some candy," said a quiet little voice.

"What?" we said together. Peace, Ike, and I all looked at Patience. I had no idea she'd been paying attention to what we were talking about.

"Throw some candy. You know, like a *peen-yada*. Everybody crawls for candy," Patience said slowly, and shrugged. Her eyes never left the window.

"Huh," I said thoughtfully. "A piñata . . . that's not a bad idea, Pay-Pay. Umm . . . thanks, guys."

"You're welcome," they all said at once.

I'd have to be really crazy to start flinging candy at people.

Then again, my Secret Keeper Girl sister, Toni, had a huge smile on her face.

49

Yузi's False Alarm

CHAPTER 6

Cloudy with a Chance of Candy Showers

Toni and I waited till lunch on Monday, when there would be the most people all together in one place. We walked to a spot where there weren't any tables. Kids were everywhere, and no one was paying any attention to us.

"Ya know," said Toni, "there's just one thing I have to say before we start this crazy stuff."

"What?" I asked, annoyed at the delay.

"Well," she went on, "as your Secret Keeper sister, I have to tell you the truth. Sometimes the bad guy gets away."

She just let that hang out there in between us, like a UFO, and waited for me to freak. "Are you prepared to deal with it if you don't ever find out who did this?" she asked.

I raised my left eyebrow and she just shrugged her shoulders.

I reached into the bag I'd brought with me. Toni reached into her backpack. We both grabbed as much candy as we could hold in our hands, keeping them concealed in the bags. I nodded and we threw the candy straight up, as high as humanly possible into the airspace that was the Rutherford B. Hayes Middle School cafeteria. I watched the next moments unfold in what seemed like slow motion. Red hot fireballs, a rainbow of jawbreakers, caramel squares, Blo-Pops, and individually wrapped Twizzlers sailed through the air. As they rained back down, I heard someone say, "Ow!! My eye! Something hit my eye!"

I was pretty sure it was a jawbreaker.

Then another kid yelled, "It's raining candy-y-y!!!"

Originally, my goal was to get out of the way and check out as many shoe soles as possible while everyone was crawling around grabbing candy . . . but it never happened.

As I backed away, an eager candy diver accidentally tripped me. My feet flew out in front of me, and I was in the air for just a second before sitting hard on the floor.

If I'm learning anything in this new town, it's how to wipe out!

Whatever candy was left in my bag dumped out, causing more chaos. I looked up just in time to see a girl get elbowed in the back. She was holding milk and

52

fruit punch. Both her drinks tipped over and I was suddenly covered in a frothy mixture of pink liquid.

"My hair!" I wailed.

I was sitting there, sputtering and wiping my eyes, when someone else slipped and landed in a heap on top of me. *Oooff!*

It was Toni.

Gasping for air, we dug ourselves out of the candy war zone before anything else could go wrong. My eyes were stinging, my clothes were stained, and fruit-punch flavored milk was still making its way through my tight curls and down my face.

This had been a bad idea.

Toni walked me to the girls' room so I could clean up. I looked in the mirror to see pink drizzles still dripping from my hair. My hoodie was drenched, too. I pulled it off over my head.

"That was crazy back there!" she said, but I could tell she loved it.

I wanted to laugh, but the whole thing wasn't very funny yet—maybe in a few minutes. Right now, all I could think of was how sore and sticky I was. My orange Chucks stuck to the floor.

Kate and Danika just happened to pop in to the same bathroom.

"Wow!" said Kate. "You've been slimed! What happened?"

We explained.

"It was cool!" said Toni.

"Yeah?" asked Danika. "It's going to be real cool if our club gets shut down and we all end up in detention again for causing mass chaos with candy in the cafeteria!"

We all giggled at how that sounded.

"Seriously, Yuzi," said Kate. "You might want to take this whole revenge thing a little less seriously."

No one said anything, but everyone was fussing over me. Danika was fixing my hair. Toni was wiping my shoes with a wet brown paper towel.

GO TO secretkeepergirl.com and type in the secret word "Hair" to see Yuzi's favorite hairstyles!

"I've got an extra hoodie in my backpack," offered Kate. She pulled it out and handed it to me. Then the bell rang.

We dashed out of the bathroom to make it to class.

On the way, I balled up my soggy hoodie and put it in my locker. *That's going to smell wonderful later,* I thought. At the bottom of my locker, next to some books, lay an innocent-looking caramel square candy.

I looked at it and said, "Nooooo, thank you!" And I firmly shut and locked the long metal door, imprisoning the evil little confection.

No matter what my Secret Keeper friends said, I wanted to find "the bad guy," as Toni had called him, and lock him up.

There's got to be a better way to find that shoe! I thought.

Yuzi's False Alarm

CHAPTER 7

Discovering Secret Shark Teeth

"Yum! Banana berry!" I said, sniffing the yummy gloss I was putting on my lips.

It was the end of our first SKG club meeting. Toni had come late, but when she had finally arrived, Danika called the meeting to order. She went over the club rules we had so far, including the one about only wearing banana berry lipgloss. Kate presented us all with our first tube.

Even though the jury was still out on whether I liked Marion, Ohio, I knew I was going to like this club. I smacked my lips.

About then Danika slipped out of the classroom with something from Mrs. V. *Probably delivering something to the office,* I thought. Mrs. V walked toward the rest of us.

"I have an idea," she said. "Why don't each of you grab a piece of paper and draw a picture that shows how you feel about life right now?" She was just way too deep of a thinker for me sometimes. All I wanted to do was talk to my Secret Keeper Girl sisters about how to find the guy who'd gotten me into detention.

We all just stared at her until Kate said, "I don't get it, Mrs. V. What do you mean?"

Mrs. V smiled. "Well, I know that if something's really bothering me, sometimes it helps me to use art to express my feelings about it. For example, after my cat got sick and died, I was really sad and I missed her a lot. So I painted a picture of her sleeping in her favorite spot and it actually made me feel better."

"I think I get it," said Toni. "But I'm not sure I'm that great at drawing stuff."

"You don't have to be," Mrs. V said. "It's not about winning a contest or anything. It's just for *you*."

"I think it's a great idea, Mrs. V!" I said. "I've totally run out of ideas for finding the guy who pulled the fire alarm. Maybe this will help me think of the perfect way to find him!"

We all grabbed some paper and things to draw with.

Staring at the blank paper in front of me, I concentrated really hard on what I should draw to describe what I'm feeling.

A shoe? No. I'm tired of shoes.

A cob of corn? Definitely **not**.

Aha! I know!

I laid all the colored pencils out and started sketching.

A few minutes later, Mrs. V said, "Does anyone want to show the rest of us what you sketched?"

I shot my hand up and said, "Me! I'll go first!"

"Okay, Yuzi. Go right ahead," Mrs. V said as she sat on her desk.

I took a deep breath, held up my picture, and said, "I drew a picture of a judge, who kind of looks like Principal Butter. He's pointing down at me and saying, 'Yuzi! Mrs. Chickory thinks you pulled the fire alarm, so here's a pink slip!' That's me down there and I'm saying, 'I didn't do it! Why doesn't anyone believe me?!' And that's Danika, Kate, and Toni dressed as super-hero detectives and you're all saying, 'Don't worry, Yuzi! The Secret Keeper Girls will save you!' I'm sorry, Mrs. V, but I didn't have time to put you in the picture yet."

"Very good, Yuzi, and you really are a talented artist!" Mrs. V said. She clapped for me, and Toni and Kate joined in.

"But, Yuzi," Mrs. V said. "Let me ask you something."

"'kay," I said.

"Didn't you say you nailed some kid in the cafeteria in the eye with a jawbreaker a couple days ago?" she said.

"Well, yeah," I said. "I sure did."

We laughed.

"Did you find that kid and tell them it was you who did it?" she asked.

"Well, no," I said. "I didn't mean to . . . it just got out of control . . . it was totally crazy."

We were all quiet.

"Sometimes, things 'get out of control,'" said Mrs. V. I got kind of a heavy feeling in my stomach like I get when I eat too many of my mom's famous meat pies. Only, my stomach felt empty, too. It wasn't a good feeling. For the first time, I considered the fact that maybe, just maybe, the guy who pulled the fire alarm didn't mean to pin it on me.

"Okay, who else? Toni?"

Toni sat up and said, "Fine, but don't laugh at my drawing!"

We all promised we wouldn't laugh.

Before Toni showed her picture, she said, "I drew a picture of the stupid 'secret' symbol the football players write on everything. It's always been my dream to kick for the football team, so that's why I drew it. It's supposed to look like the open mouth of a shark. See?"

When she held up her picture, I couldn't believe my eyes.

"Whoa! Whoa! **Whoa!**" I was practically screaming. "That's it! That's the symbol thingy I saw on the guy's shoe! I'm almost positive!"

"What? *This*?" asked Toni.

On her paper, she had drawn a circle. All along the inside edge, there were little spikes pointing toward the center of the circle. It sort of looked like a reverse sun.

Kate looked at me. "Are you sure it's what you saw, Yuzi?"

"Could you draw it again with a white pencil on black paper?" I asked Toni.

Kate grabbed a white pencil, and Mrs. V got some black paper. As Toni started drawing again, we watched closely.

When she finished, she held up the paper. I backed up to the opposite end of the art room so I could see the symbol from a distance.

"I'm pretty sure that's it," I said to the girls.

"That narrows it down to the football team," Toni said.

"Well, at least now I have a better idea whose shoes to look at," I said.

"Yuzi!" Toni said. "You might actually have a chance to find this guy!"

I immediately came up with a brilliant plan.

"I've got it!" I squealed.

Our school was having a massive roller-skating party tonight, and they needed volunteers for a whole list of things. I remembered seeing a sign-up list earlier in the day. It was on the bulletin board right outside of Mrs. V's room.

I dashed out the door followed by Toni, Kate, and Mrs. V. I searched for the words "Shoe check counter" on the list. Since they needed two students to help, Toni could do it with me. I giggled at the thought of having hundreds of shoes pass through our hands for our inspection. Oh, the power!

"Isn't it so deliciously *perfect*!?" I asked Toni. "All the kids in the school will be handing us their shoes and we'll give them their roller skates!"

"I'll finally be able to pick out my own skates," Toni said with a sound of relief.

"What are you talking about?" I asked.

"Whenever I get skates from a rink, I have to yell out my size over and over, partly because it's so loud at rinks, and partly because they can't believe what size I'm asking for. It's really annoying. This time, I won't have to deal with that," Toni explained.

I looked down at Toni's long feet and smiled. "I'm happy for you. And I'm glad you got that off your chest. There won't be anything distracting you from our important mission," I said with pretend seriousness.

65

She swatted at me. I ducked but she hit me on the side of my head anyway.

"Well, Yuzi, let's get '*rolling*'! Get it? We're going *roller-skating* . . ." Toni said, making herself laugh.

I laughed, too. "Sure, Toni. Let's get '*rolling*'!"

I'd forgotten everything Mrs. V had just said moments ago. I was ready to confront the guy who'd ruined my life at the ZoomAround Skating Rink that night.

Yuzi's False Alarm

CHAPTER 8

Sole Searching

"Anything yet?" I yelled to Toni. We were taking shoes and handing back skates as fast as we could.

Toni and I were at opposite ends of the counter. Two parent chaperones worked with us, but they were more interested in gossiping about the Popcorn Festival.

Toni shook her head. "Nope. Nada!"

We'd been flipping every black-soled sneaker for the last thirty minutes, checking for the symbol. Flip and check, flip and check. We only had ten minutes left before we switched with the other people who had counter duty.

The skating rink was packed. Everywhere you looked, there were parents and chaperones and students eating, drinking, skating, or falling. The music was so loud, you could almost feel your eyeballs quiver in their sockets. Colored lights danced across the roller-skating floor.

The rush began to die down and I walked over to Toni. "What if he isn't here?" I moaned, sipping on a soda.

"There are still a lot of kids who haven't gotten skates yet," she said.

"I know, but we're off in less than five minutes."

"Yeah, but we'll be on again at the end of the night, when everyone'll be getting their shoes back," Toni said. "We can keep checking then and see if we missed anything while we were gone."

Toni and I put on skates as the next group of volunteers arrived. We clomped our way along the rubber-floored outer rink in search of Kate and Danika. We found Kate eating potato chips.

"Danika's skating," she told us.

"I want to skate," I said. "But not till I use the bathroom first."

"I'm trying to finish this bag of chips before I go out there. I'll come with you," Kate said.

Toni said, "I'll be out on the floor when you guys get back."

"Okay," Kate and I said together.

On the way to the bathroom, I saw Trevor. It's hard to miss that red hair, even in dim lighting. The skates he was wearing made him look so much taller and thinner. He was too far away to talk to, so I waved. He kind of half-waved back. I was glad Toni wasn't with me.

Kate shook her head. "That's funny how Toni can't stand Trevor, but you think he's fine," she said.

"He's okay," I said.

When it was our turn behind the counter again, there was almost no one getting skates.

"I can't give up now! I'm so close!" I said desperately. "I'm going to check for any sneakers that might have come in while we were out." I began going through all the shelves of shoes again.

Toni shrugged. "Guess I'll help. We don't have anything else to do. Besides, there doesn't seem to be that many black-soled shoes."

We started looking, and in only a few minutes, I found the symbol.

"Here they are! Here they are!" I shouted, nearly falling off the chair I was standing on.

Toni ran over to see.

The sneakers were black and white basketball shoes with a thin striping of blue up the sides. I couldn't believe I'd found them!

"That's a pretty sad-looking symbol," she said as we both looked at a pathetic version of the football players' secret sign.

"Yeah. And these shoes reek like . . . nachos!" I said, holding my nose.

"What on earth has you girls so involved over there?" said a familiar voice.

Mrs. Chickory! She must have switched with one of the chaperones while we were looking at shoes. I swallowed hard.

Looking more ostrich-like than ever in the narrow space behind the counter, she came over to see what we were looking at. She was not impressed.

"Why don't you girls go out there and skate? There's nothing to do here, and we have a little while before the closing rush," she said.

"No thanks," I said.

"We're fine," said Toni.

"Well, fine then," Mrs. Chickory continued. "How about this? Why don't you girls go get us all some nachos?"

Still holding the shoes, nachos did not sound like a tasty suggestion to me. But she was trying hard to be pleasant.

Toni and I looked at each other as Mrs.Chickory dug her wallet out of her purse so she could hand us some money.

"Well, I'm in the mood for nachos," she said. "Here's some money. I'll even treat you girls. Well, how about it?" She stood there on her tiny feet and held out the cash. Was it possible the angry ostrich was being generous?

I took a deep breath and blew it out. "Uhhh . . . okay, Mrs. Chickory," I said, and slowly took the money from her hand. "We'll go get the nachos. But it's super, *super* important that we know whose shoes these are," I pleaded. "Could you maybe make sure that you get a good look at whoever picks them up, if they come before we get back? Maybe even get their name?"

"Tracking down a particular *gentleman*, are we?" Mrs. Chickory asked in a disapproving tone. Then she smiled.

I tried very hard not to roll my eyes.

"Actually, no," Toni said. "But it really is important."

"Well, I'll see what I can do, girls," Mrs. Chickory said with a laugh. "Now, skedaddle! Get those nachos!"

The nacho line was crazy long. I kept staring at the roller skate shaped clock. We were gone for almost fifteen minutes! When we got back to the shoe check counter, my worst fear had come true. The shoes were gone! And so was Mrs. Chickory.

"Where are the shoes?" I wailed. "And where's Mrs. Chickory?"

"What shoes?" asked Bobby. He's the actual shoe check guy who works for the rink, and he was wearing a ridiculously bright yellow ZoomAround T-shirt.

"Where's Mrs. Chickory?" I asked again.

Bobby was annoyed. He wiped his nose with the back of his hand, sniffed, then glared at me. "Some kid fell and she went to get some bandages or something. What's it to *you*?"

"Did you return some shoes?" I asked him, trying not to freak out.

He looked at me like he'd never heard a more stupid question in all of his life.

"Ah . . . yeah!" he answered, his voice rising.

"Did you happen to notice who you gave them to?" I asked.

Bobby put down the can of deodorant he'd been spraying into skates.

Looking at us, he said, "Listen, little junior higher and really tall junior higher, go away!" He put on his headphones and went back to spraying the skates.

He was a little cranky, so I stopped asking questions.

But I thought I might cry. I was surprised to see that Toni was grinning mischievously. She held up something in her hand, waggling it. It was a bright pink marker.

"Wha—?" I started.

"Danika and Kate called a super-secret Secret Keeper Girl meeting right before the skating party. We devised a plan to mark the shoe if we found it without its owner," she said smugly, raising an eyebrow. "So, I marked it right before we left for nachos. Just in case we didn't get back in time."

"You marked the shoe?" I asked in shock.

"Yep," she said. "A teeny weeny pink heart on the white part of the back of the shoe. So now we don't need to see the bottom of it!"

"You so **rock!**" I said, extremely relieved. Then I shouted, "Why didn't you say anything?" and swatted her arm.

"You were too busy falling apart," Toni said with a laugh.

I yanked a green flip-flop off the shelf and threw it at her. I missed but I didn't care.

I was starting to feel like a regular Sherlock Holmes. Nancy Drew, maybe! The Secret Keeper Girls were one step closer to exposing the true fire-alarm puller.

Yuzi's False Alarm

CHAPTER 9

Truth and Oatmeal Brains

"Fire alarms are red. You don't have a clue. You'd better run or I'll flatten you!"

Danika, Kate, and Toni laughed and rolled their eyes.

Kate said, "No offense, Yuzi, but you can't say something that rhymes when you catch the guy. He'll just laugh in your face!" Everyone else agreed.

"Yeah," said Danika. "Why don't you try something more witty like, 'You *alarmed* me. Now I'll *alarm* you!'"

A moment of silence, and then total laughter.

Toni interrupted. "You guys are all thinking like wimps. Yuzi, you need to say something with authority and demand! You've won the battle! Victory is yours for the taking!"

"Okay," I said. "What if I go up to him from behind, poke him in the back and say, '*Reeeeach for the skiiiiies!*'"

Toni looked shocked. "Are you kidding? Have you *looked* at yourself? You are no cowgirl!"

"I think I'll know exactly what to say or do as soon as I lay eyes on that snake," I said with confidence. "All I want is to see his face and prove to everyone that I'm not crazy or a liar, *and* I want to tell him what I think of him for letting me take the punishment for something I didn't do."

"I totally get that you need to know who it was so you're not blamed," said Danika. "But, let's be real. It's not like all the scenes you see in movies about someone telling off the bad guy really happen in real life."

We sat in silence and for the first time I wondered if this thing would end with a quick exchange of wit like I'd imagined.

"You could always just forgive him," piped up Kate.

I could feel my face drop. I felt a little twinge of anger flare up inside of me. It was the same feeling I had every time I thought of meeting this mystery boy. I was hoping that it would stop once I knew who it was and told him what I thought.

But I wasn't sure.

"It's just an idea," Kate said and shrugged her shoulders.

On my way to science, I tried to come up with some more creative things I could say when I find him.

Suddenly, my mom's voice crept into my head saying, "I'm sure whoever did it knows they did the wrong thing. It's quite possible that they feel bad but are too frightened to confess."

I pushed the thought out of my head and kept working on lines.

"Hey, you're not just on the shark team. You are a shark!"

Somehow, I didn't feel much better saying that. That's when it occurred to me. Not just my mom, but everyone I knew in Marion, Ohio—granted I didn't know many—had said I should just let the poor guy off the hook. Mrs. V had said it. Toni had mentioned it before we threw candy. Even Danika and Kate had mentioned it today.

Maybe they were right.

Maybe it'd feel better if I just **forgave** the guy.

Mr. Picadilly was a few minutes late—again. It only takes a few seconds for a teacherless class to go wild, especially when it happens over and over. Already, someone was up front doing a bad impression of Mr. Picadilly. Everybody else was talking, or standing, or both.

I turned to my left and said, "Hey, Trev."

"Hey," he said.

Sometimes he acts a little grumpy and hardly looks at me, and then I can see why he and Toni don't get along. But most of the time, he's pretty nice. To me, anyway.

"Awww, c'mon!" he suddenly wailed, looking down.

"What?" I asked, startled.

"Stupid!" Trevor said, and he angrily sat back hard in his chair and sort of started pouting.

"What's the matter?" I asked. *What is his problem? This must be the Trevor Toni knows.*

He looked at the classroom door, then quickly got up and went to Mr. Picadilly's desk. It only took him a second to grab the white-out and sit back down.

"Some idiot must have . . ." He was mumbling, so I didn't hear the rest. He shook the bottle hard as he popped off a shoe. My mouth went dry.

"Why would some dumb person do this?" he asked, half-whining. He unscrewed the little white cap. "It was probably a stupid girl!"

"Do what?" I barely squeaked, heart pounding.

He picked up his shoe and jabbed the heel at my face. "That!" he said.

I was nose-to-nose with a little pink heart. My brains turned to oatmeal.

As Trevor began to carefully paint white-out over the heart, I could see the bottom of the shoe—and the unavoidable truth: the Shark symbol—faded and lopsided, but oh so clear. It hit me like a brick in the head, and all my clever smack-talk evaporated. Trevor Kenworth pulled the fire alarm!

"What's the matter with you?" he asked.

My breath was coming in short gasps. I turned to look at him and opened my mouth to say something. But my tongue had gone numb.

"What do you *mean*, your tongue went numb?! How could you not say anything?" bellowed Toni. "I mean, it was *Trevor Kenworth*!"

I'd met her, Danika, and Kate in the library later and filled them in on what happened with Trevor. Toni was practically yelling, so the librarian gave a firm "Ssshhhhh!" from her desk.

"I should have known it was him!" Toni continued more quietly. "That reptile!"

"I can't believe he's been talking to you and stuff, knowing you're the one who got in trouble instead of him," Danika whispered.

"All this time I thought it was really nice of him to not talk about the fire alarm. Now I know it was just because he felt guilty," I said in a barely-there voice. "I'm so mad!" Although it's hard to *sound* mad when you're whispering.

"What are you going to do?" asked Danika.

"I'm not really sure yet," I said.

"You *have* to tell Principal Butter, Yuzi," Toni said.

I nodded my head. "I know, but I want to talk to Trevor first and tell him that I know he pulled that alarm."

"When are you going to do it?" Kate whispered.

"I don't know. Tomorrow, maybe?" I said. "I won't really see him again today."

"Well, as your Secret Keeper Girl sisters, we expect a full report," Danika said.

"When I didn't know who did it, it was a lot easier to think about revenge. But it's totally different now that I know it was Trevor. I mean, we're kind of like almost friends and his mom's super-nice," I said in his defense.

"There's a football scrimmage today after school," Toni said suddenly. "Do you want us to pelt him with rotten fruit?"

"Ooooh! We totally should!" said Kate, bouncing in her seat.

"Great idea," I joked. "Got any watermelons?"

I pictured Trevor covered in smelly fruit guts, running for his life. Even though I knew it would never happen, it made me smile.

Yuzi's False Alarm

CHAPTER 10

A Weasely Chicken

After a good night's sleep, I woke up ready to face Trevor in science class. Only one problem—he wasn't there.

Maybe he knows I know and is scared to come to class, I thought. I was glad he wasn't there. I still wasn't sure what to say to him.

My thoughts were interrupted by the *beeeeep* of the intercom.

The secretary's voice came squeaking into the classroom. "Mr. Picadilly, would you please have Yuzi Ukachi come to the front office?"

"I'll send her down," Mr. Picadilly responded. Then he turned to me and said, "You can give me your homework later."

I left the classroom as several voices sang out, "Busted!" Mr. Picadilly was telling them all to shush as the door swung shut behind me.

Great! *Now* what am I being accused of?

"Have a seat," the secretary told me as soon as I arrived. But I had only just started to lower myself into the chair when Principal Butter opened his door and said, "Yuzi, would you come in please?"

I walked into his office. This room held no good memories for me.

Sue Kenworth turned her red head to look at me. *What is she doing in here?* Trevor was sitting next to her, head drooped. Mrs. Kenworth gave me a sad smile as Principal Butter said, "Well, Yuzi, it seems there's some apologizing to be done."

Mrs. Kenworth and Principal Butter explained that Trevor was the one who pulled the fire alarm, which I had already figured out. I kept glancing at Trevor. He looked like a helium balloon five days after a party, and it was obvious he'd been crying. The more the adults said, the lower he slumped in his seat. It was hard to stay mad at him as he wilted like steamed spinach.

When they had finished, Mrs. Kenworth said, "Trevor, go ahead."

Trevor took a deep breath, but didn't raise his head. "I'm sorry," he mumbled.

"Oh, you'd better do better than that, young man," his mom said sharply.

"I'm sorry I let you get in trouble for pulling the fire alarm." He finally looked up. "And I'm sorry for acting like a . . ."

"Weasel," Mrs. Kenworth filled in.

Trevor frowned at his mom. ". . . weasel, and being too . . ."

"Chicken," she prompted.

Trevor sighed again. " . . . too chicken to take responsibility for what I did."

I stood there for a second, not knowing what to say. I thought about how angry and upset I had been the last time I was in this room. I thought about Trevor talking to me in class and then about him sitting here like a dejected blob, and I realized everyone had been right. Staying mad wouldn't make anything better. It would only make *me* feel worse.

"It's no big deal, Trevor," I said. "I mean, I can't believe you were going to try to get away with it, but I'll try not to stay mad at you. By the way," I added. "I knew it was you. I figured it out yesterday when you were covering up the heart on your shoe."

"You're the one who did that?" Trevor asked.

85

"No," I said, thinking of how my *Secret Keeper Girl Club* had come up with that one without me. "But it helped prove it was you." I left Toni out of it, not wanting to make things between them worse than they already were.

A few minutes later, after Trevor and Mrs. Kenworth had left, Principal Butter said, "So, Yuzi. It turns out you did see someone in that hall after all. I've called your parents, and I've also let Mrs. Chickory know that we've found who really did it." He looked me in the eyes. "I'm sorry I gave you detention for something you did not do. And I hope we didn't completely destroy your opinion of our school. It was a hard way to start the year." *No kidding.*

After school, I explained the details of how Trevor got caught as Kate, Danika, and Toni huddled around me in our Secret Keeper Girl hangout, Mrs. V's room. She was listening, too.

"Apparently, since he played so terribly last night, some of the guys on his team were yelling at him in the parking lot later," I said.

"One of the guys told Trevor that he'd have to do more

than pull a stupid fire alarm if he wanted to prove he could kick better than a girl." I looked at Toni and laughed. "I guess they were talking about you. Anyway, they didn't know Trevor's mom was in the car nearby. She heard the boys, jumped out of the car, and flipped out on them!"

We all laughed, imagining Mrs. Kenworth, with her crazy red hair, ripping into a bunch of middle school football players.

"They probably almost wet themselves!" Kate laughed.

"Well, I guess Trevor got suspended for a few days," I said.

"It's about time!" Toni said.

"Score one for the *Secret Keeper Girl Club!* Woo hoo!" Danika squealed, jumping up and down.

"Yeah," I said kind of quietly. "Only the weird thing is, I thought it would feel really good when Trevor got caught and punished."

"Are you saying you feel *sorry* for *him*?" Toni asked.

I looked down at my hands. "Not exactly. It's like, I know he needs to be punished for what he did, but he was really broken up about it when he was apologizing . . . like he really meant it."

Kate said, "That's pretty cool, Yuzi. He could have been a real jerk about it. Come to think of it, you could have been a real jerk about it, too, but you weren't."

Mrs. V finally spoke up. "Sometimes what we think will feel good in the moment isn't actually what will satisfy us as time goes on. Forgiveness is always better than sitting and waiting for someone to get what we think they deserve."

I nodded my head. "I guess that's what my mom was trying to get into my brain all along. You know, there's lots of times where my parents just don't get it, but sometimes they're actually right."

"You know, Yuzi, you *could* tell your mom that. It might make her feel good," Mrs. V said.

"Yeah. Maybe I will. Anyway, thanks, guys, for helping me with everything," I said. "I couldn't have done it without my Secret Keeper Girls!"

Toni said, "No problema!" Then we piled into a group hug.

As we started talking about other things, I pulled a notebook out of my schoolbag. Something fell out. It was my "List of Terribles."

I looked it over, thinking how much better things are now. It had finally been proven that I didn't pull the alarm. I have real friends who care about me and believed me when other people didn't. And I'm not feeling quite as bad about moving here.

So now I'm making a new list, a "List of Wonderfuls." Dumb title, I know. But I can't think of another word for the opposite of "terribles."

The first thing on my new list is the same as the first thing on my old list: Moving to Marion, Ohio.

Okay, so maybe I'm not going to hate this town.

List of Wonderfuls!

Girl Gab About Forgiveness

Hello, Secret Keeper Girl! Hope you had a blast reading about Yuzi and her insane quest to solve the mystery of the real fire alarm puller. As you may have noticed, she also learned about forgiveness. Did you? Let's talk about it.

> "Bear with each other and forgive whatever grievances you may have against one another. Forgive as the Lord forgave you."
> Colossians 3:13

Gab About It:

Hopefully, you can see that verse in the pages of *Yuzi's False Alarm!* Let's look at it really closely together.

💜 Maybe you've heard of someone "bearing" a heavy backpack at school. With that in mind, what does it mean to "bear with each other and forgive"?......................................

....

....

💜 Can you think of a time that your mom or someone close to you did this for you when you needed forgiveness?

....

....

....

💜 For most of the book, Yuzi did not respond the way God wants us to in this verse. How was she acting? ....

....

....

....

💜 At the end, what did Yuzi find out when she finally decided to forgive?..

....

....

....

💜 Is there someone like Trevor in your life? Someone you need to forgive? What do you think God wants you to do?

....

....

....

PRAY IT OUT LOUD! One thing Yuzi learned for sure is that it's good to get advice from your mom and dad, your friends (Danika, Kate, and Toni), and even your teachers (Mrs. V) when you've been wronged! It would be awesome if you could take a minute to pray with your mom about the "Trevor" in your life. Ask her advice on what to do. Ask God to give you the grace to live Colossians 3:13.

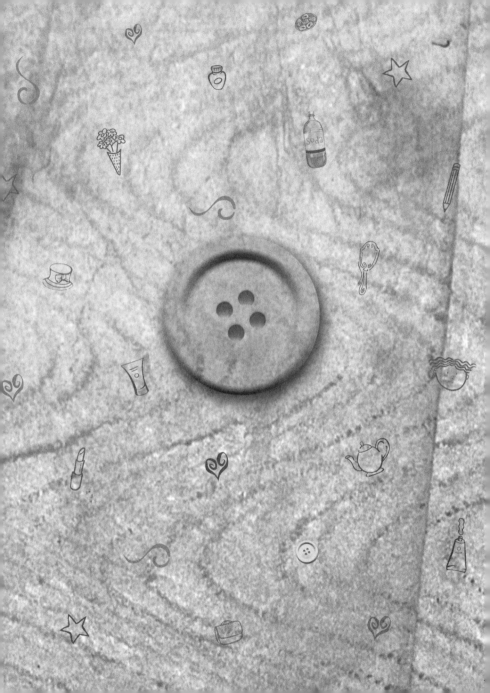

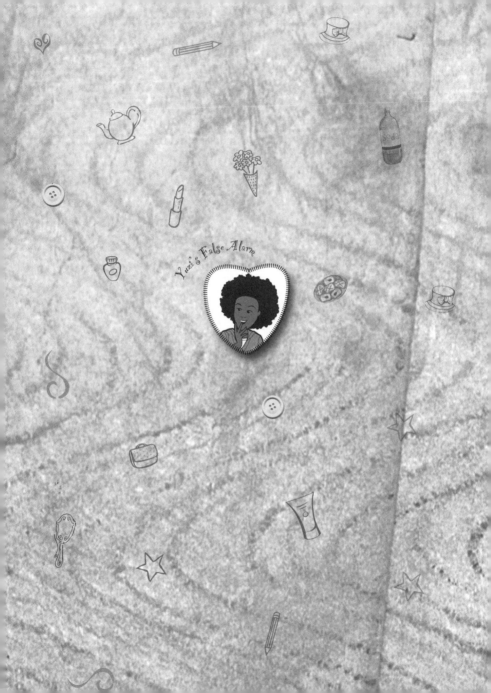

Yuzi's False Alarm

MORE

SeCret Keeper GiRL
FICTION SERIES

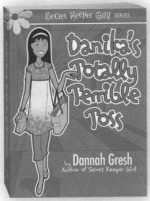

ISBN-13: 978-0-8024-8702-5

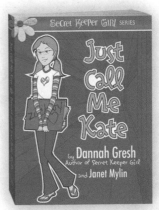

ISBN-13: 978-0-8024-8703-2

ISBN-13: 978-0-8024-8704-9

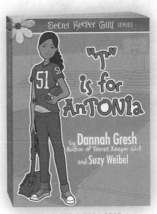

ISBN-13: 978-0-8024-8705-6

MORE

Secret Keeper Girl

ISBN-13: 978-0-8024-3121-9

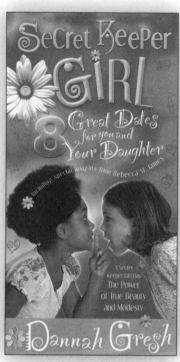

ISBN-13: 978-0-8024-8700-1

The most fun Moms and daughters will ever have digging into God's Word.